'Twas The Night Before Christmas

Illustrated by Greg Hildebrandt

'Twas The Night Before Christmas

Illustrated by Greg Hildebrandt

BARNES
&NOBLE
BOOKS
NEW YORK

'Twas

the night before Christmas,

When all through the house,

Not a creature was stirring,

Not even a mouse.

The stockings were hung

By the chimney with care,

In hopes that St. Nicholas

Soon would be there.

he

Children were nestled

All snug in their beds,

While visions of sugarplums

Danced in their heads.

And Mamma in her kerchief,

And I in my cap,

Had just settled down

For a long winter's nap.

When out on the lawn

There arose such a clatter,

I sprang from my bed

To see what was the matter.

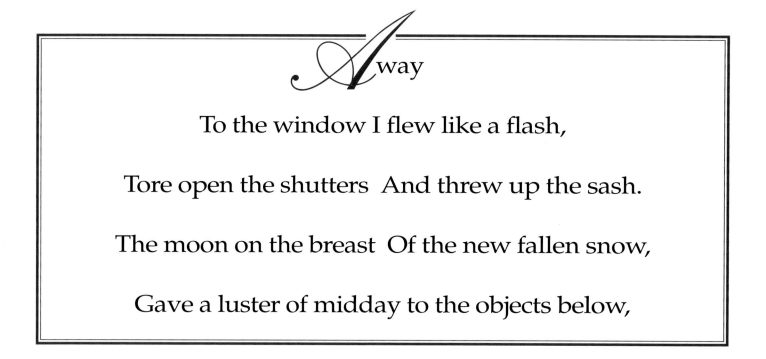

$\mathscr{A}$way

To the window I flew like a flash,

Tore open the shutters And threw up the sash.

The moon on the breast Of the new fallen snow,

Gave a luster of midday to the objects below,

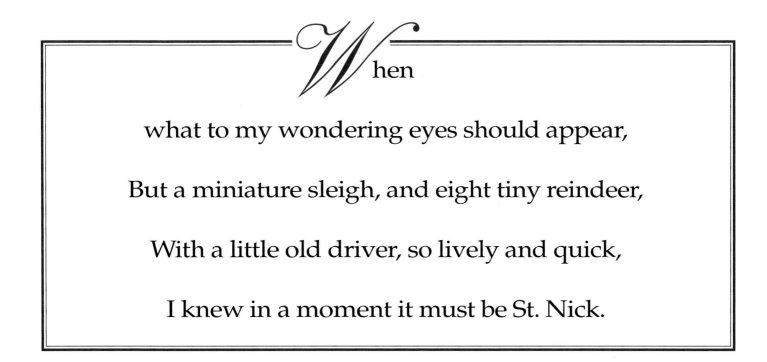

When

what to my wondering eyes should appear,

But a miniature sleigh, and eight tiny reindeer,

With a little old driver, so lively and quick,

I knew in a moment it must be St. Nick.

More

Rapid than eagles

His coursers they came,

And he whistled, and shouted,

And called them by name:

"Now, Dasher! Now, Dancer!

Now, Prancer and Vixen!

On, Comet! On, Cupid!

On, Donder and Blitzen!

To the top of the porch!

To the top of the wall!

Now, dash away! Dash away!

Dash away all!"

_A_s

Dry leaves that before the wild hurricane fly,

When they meet with an obstacle, mount to the sky,

So up to the housetop the coursers they flew,

With the sleigh full of toys, and St. Nicholas, too.

*A*nd

Then in a twinkling, I heard on the roof

The prancing and pawing of each little hoof.

As

I drew in my head, And was turning around,

Down the chimney St. Nicholas Came with a bound.

He was dressed all in fur, From his head to his foot,

And his clothes were all tarnished With ashes and soot.

A bundle of toys He had flung on his back,

And he looked like a peddler Just opening his pack.

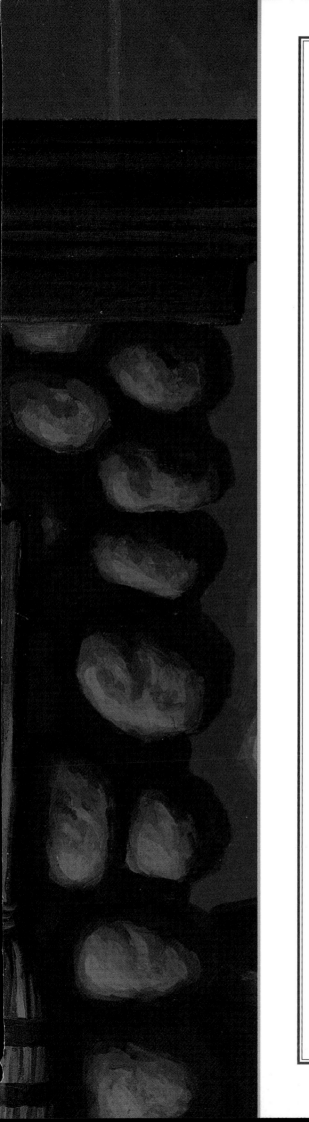

His Eyes how they twinkled!

His dimples how merry!

His cheeks were like roses,

His nose like a cherry.

His droll little mouth

Was drawn up like a bow,

And the beard on his chin

Was as white as the snow.

The stump of a pipe

He held tight in his teeth,

And the smoke, it encircled

His head like a wreath.

He had a broad face

And a little round belly,

That shook, when he laughed,

Like a bowl full of jelly.

_H_e

Was chubby and plump,

A right jolly old elf,

And I laughed when I saw him,

In spite of myself.

A wink of his eye

And a twist of his head,

Soon gave me to know

I had nothing to dread.

He spoke not a word,

But went straight to his work,

And filled all the stockings,

Then turned with a jerk,

And laying a finger aside of his nose,

And giving a nod

Up the chimney he rose.

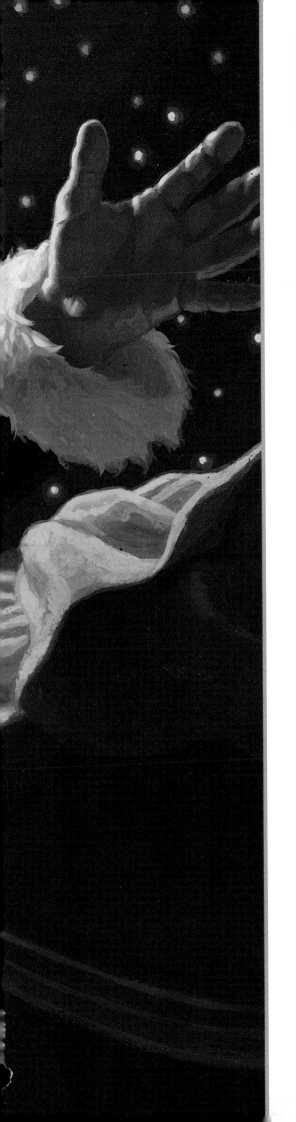

$\mathcal{H}$e

Sprang to his sleigh,

To his team gave a whistle,

And away they all flew

Like the down of a thistle.

But I heard him exclaim

As he drove out of sight,

"Happy Christmas to all,

And to all a good night."

Jingle bells, jingle bells, jingle all the way,
Oh what fun it is to ride in a one horse open sleigh!

ABOUT THE AUTHOR

C. Clement Moore was born in 1779 in New York, and was, for many years, a noted professor of religion, having published several scholarly works. But it is for his light-hearted children's poem, *An Account of a Visit from St. Nicholas*, published for the first time in 1823, for which he is best known and loved.

As the legend goes, on the night before Christmas Day, 1822, Professor Moore had just returned from shopping, anxious to warm himself by the fire in his study. As he sat, he began to write the poem that began, "Twas the night before Christmas,/when all through the house..." From that moment on, Christmas, especially for children and their parents, would never be the same.

Apparently, Moore had never intended his work to be for any audience beyond his own children. The poem was originally published anonymously in the newspaper *The Troy Sentinel*, and is believed to have been submitted to the paper by a member of Moore's family without his knowledge.

While the poem was widely reprinted, it was not credited to Moore until 1837, when it was published in a collection of his poetry. The poem, now known by its famous opening lines, *'Twas the Night Before Christmas*, was originally published in book form in 1848. Moore's classic has delighted generations of children and their parents. Probably more than any other piece of secular literature, *'Twas* has defined the mood and expression of Christmas.

Deck the halls with boughs of holly,
Fa - la - la - la - la,   la - la - la - la
'Tis the season to be jolly,
Fa - la - la - la - la,   la - la - la - la

ABOUT THE ILLUSTRATOR

Greg Hildebrandt is the latest in an esteemed line of illustrators who have been inspired by C. Clement Moore's Christmas classic.

Greg's career in art began at the ripe old age of 2, when his father attempted to teach him and his twin brother Tim how to color with crayons. Soon, the twins had taken the crayons away from their father, and were even coloring within the lines.

In the past 12 years, Greg, following in the tradition of many great illustrators, has gone on to illustrate 15 of the classics and many fairy tales for children. The series includes: *The Wizard of Oz*, *Aladdin and the Magic Lamp*, *Robin Hood*, *Dracula*, and *Phantom of the Opera*. There are over 3,500,000 copies in print of his combined works.

The art of Greg Hildebrandt allows the fantasies and dreams of children of all ages to come true. His work becomes the pathway leading to the written word, igniting the desire for children and adults alike to love reading.

1996 Barnes & Noble Books   ISBN 0-7607-0377-9
Printed and bound in the United States of America
M 9 8 7 6 5 4 3 2 1
KP